@RosenTeenTalk

STRESS AND ANXIETY

Shannon Harts

ROSEN PUBLISHING
NEW YORK

Published in 2021 by The Rosen Publishing Group, Inc.
29 East 21st Street, New York, NY 10010

Copyright © 2021 by The Rosen Publishing Group, Inc.

All rights reserved. No part of this book may be reproduced in any form without permission in writing from the publisher, except by a reviewer.

First Edition

Editor: Elizabeth Krajnik
Designer: Michael Flynn
Interior Layout: Rachel Rising

Photo Credits: Cover, p.1 Rob Marmion/Shutterstock.com; Cover Cosmic_Design/Shutterstock.com; Cover, pp. 1, 6, 8, 10, 12, 16, 18, 20, 22, 24, 28, 30, 32, 34, 36, 38, 40, 42 Vitya_M/Shutterestock.com; pp. 3, 5 antoniodiaz/Shutterstock.com; pp. 3, 16 H.S. Photos/Alamy Stock Photo; pp. 3, 27 Capuski/E+/Getty Images; pp. 3, 43 WPA Pool / Pool/ Getty Images Entertainment/Getty Images; p. 6 holaillustrations/Shutterstock.com; p. 7 GaudiLab/Shuttterstock.com; p. 8 tadamichi/Shutterstock.com; p. 9 Inspiring/Shutterstock.com; p. 11 bymuratdeniz/E+/Getty Images; p. 12 Kathy Hutchins/Shutterstock.com; p. 13 DFree/Shutterstock.com; p. 15 Dragon Images/Shutterstock.com; pp. 18, 29 Monkey Business Images/Shutterstock.com; p. 19 Marian Fil/Shutterstock.com; p. 20 nelen/Shutterstock.com; p. 22 Bonezboyz/Shutterstock.com; p. 23 Samuel Borges Photography/Shutterstock.com; p. 24 Andrii Symonenko/Shutterstock.com; p. 25 serdjophoto/Shutterstock.com; p. 28 LightField Studios/Shutterstock.com; p. 30 Chanintorn.v/Shutterstock.com; p. 31 photocosmos1/Shutterstock.com; p. 32 Syuzann/Shutterstock.com; p. 33 TheVisualsYouNeed/Shutterstock.com; p. 34 Pixel-Shot/Shutterstock.com; p. 35 Martin Novak/Moment/ Getty Images; p. 36 Mayur Kakade/Moment/ Getty Images; p. 39 Tony Anderson/ DigitalVision/Getty Images; p. 40 Trueffelpix/Shutterstock.com; p. 41 Weekend Images Inc./E+/Getty Images; p. 42 LinGraphics/Shutterstock.com; p.45 aldomurillo/E+/Getty Images.

Some of the images in this book illustrate individuals who are models. The depictions do not imply actual situations or events.

Cataloging-in-Publication Data

Names: Harts, Shannon H.
Title: Stress and anxiety / Shannon H. Harts.
Description: New York : Rosen Publishing, 2021. | Series: RosenTeenTalk | Includes glossary and index.
Identifiers: ISBN 9781499468243 (pbk.) | ISBN 9781499468250 (library bound)
Subjects: LCSH: Stress in adolescence--Juvenile literature. | Stress management--Juvenile literature. | Anxiety--Juvenile literature.
Classification: LCC BF724.3.S86 H38 2021 | DDC 155.9'042--dc23

Manufactured in the United States of America

CPSIA Compliance Information: Batch #BSR20. For further information contact Rosen Publishing, New York, New York at 1-800-237-9932.

Find us on

CONTENTS

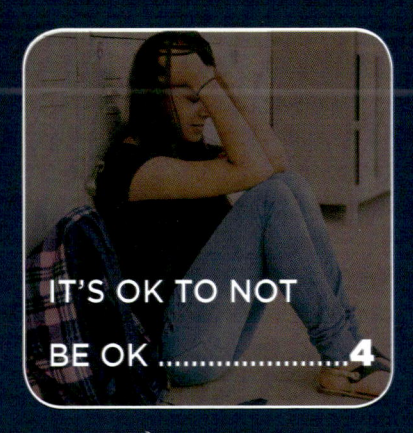

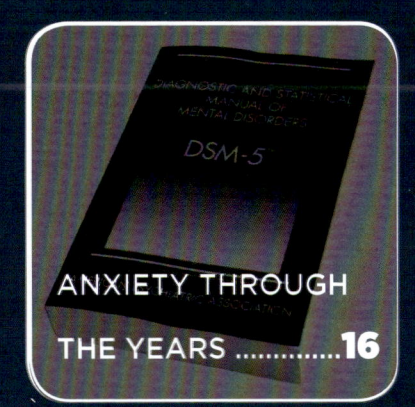

IT'S OK TO NOT BE OK 4

ANXIETY THROUGH THE YEARS 16

GETTING BETTER 26

STANDING UP TO STIGMA 42

GLOSSARY 46

INDEX 48

Chapter 1

It's OK to Not Be OK

As I wrote my name, *Madison Hamilton*, on my test, my heart started pounding. I remembered that this test is worth 25 percent of my grade. I started on the math questions. They were really hard. *I should have studied more*, I thought.

When the teacher started collecting the tests, I still had three problems left!

My breathing got faster. I felt pain in my stomach. I also started sweating. I wondered what the other students must think.

After the teacher took my test, I ran to the bathroom.

My friend Olivia followed me. She asked what was wrong. I told her about the test and about how I felt sick. She said she's felt the same. She shared how she's gotten help, starting with talking to a **psychologist**.

It's common to feel worried about taking a test. Watching yourself talk, or listening to what you say to yourself, can help. Try replacing thoughts like *I should have studied more* with something positive. One example could be: *I am prepared*.

WHAT IS STRESS?

Stress happens because of a demand or a **challenge**. This can include a test or **performance**. There's a wide range of stress symptoms, or signs. These can be physical (or felt by the body), emotional, and **cognitive**.

Over time, these symptoms can lead to more serious health issues. These can include sleep, memory, or **digestive** issues. Stress can also be chronic. "Chronic" means happening again and again. Luckily, there are many ways to get help for chronic stress.

SYMPTOMS OF STRESS

Physical Symptoms
- Shaking
- Often getting colds

Emotional Symptoms
- Being unable to quiet your mind
- Feeling like you're losing control

Cognitive Symptoms
- Being disorganized
- Being forgetful

Three Truths About Stress

1) People don't choose stress. It stems from **subconscious** beliefs about the world.

2) Problematic stress is common for teens. Around 42 percent don't think they are handling it well.

3) Stress is a big deal, and it's always OK to get help.

Leading Causes of Teen Stress

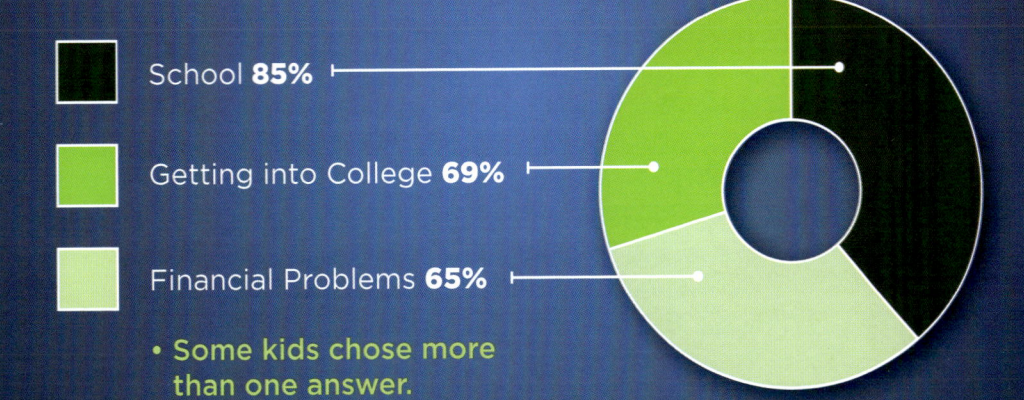

- School **85%**
- Getting into College **69%**
- Financial Problems **65%**

- Some kids chose more than one answer.

Stress 101!

This resource has worksheets and a video that can help you understand exactly how stress affects your body:
https://www.changetochill.org/about/

WHAT IS ANXIETY?

Anxiety is a little different from stress. The body's **natural** response to stress is anxiety. Anxiety is a feeling of fear about something that's going to happen. Giving a speech or going to school on your first day can cause anxious feelings.

Negative thought patterns often cause anxiety. You can challenge these thought patterns by asking yourself, "Is this really true?" This can help prevent these thoughts from taking root.

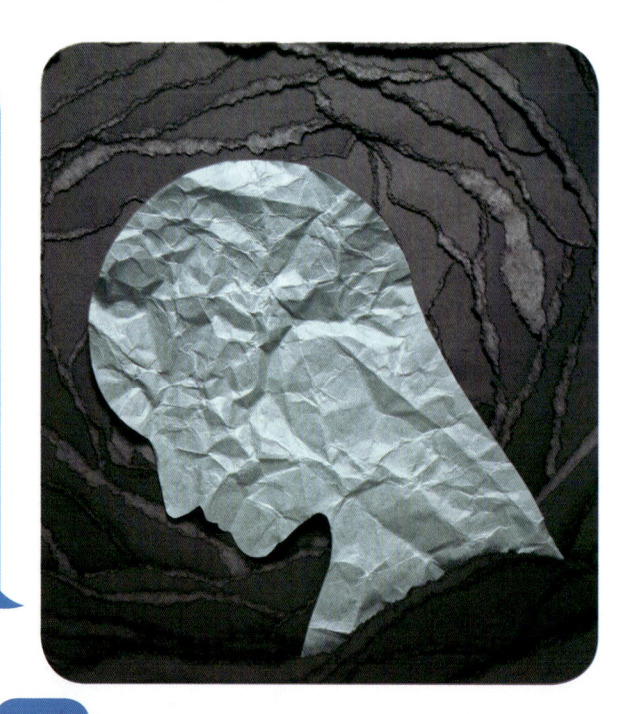

When these feelings are very strong and last a long time, you might have an anxiety disorder. Anxiety doesn't feel great, but usually people can move past it. Anxiety disorders, on the other hand, cause problems in daily life activities.

SIGNS OF ANXIETY

Behavioral Signs
- Not hanging out with friends
- Not doing things you used to enjoy
- Always asking for approval, or an OK, from adults

Emotional Signs
- Crying often
- Being afraid of making small mistakes
- Thinking too much about negative topics, or things that make you feel bad

Physical Signs
- Sudden headaches
- Sudden stomachaches
- Sleep issues

HELPFUL RESOURCES

Check out this infographic from the Anxiety and **Depression** Association of America (ADAA) website. It includes information on accepting what you can't control and staying positive:
https://adaa.org/tips-manage-anxiety-and-stress

HOW THE PROBLEMS START

Stress can become a bigger problem when it starts to cause trouble in many areas of life. **Relationships** are often one of these areas.

Stress and anxiety can make you feel like you are different from others. However, many people feel this way. About half of teens who took part in a study said someone tells them they seem stressed at least once a month. The stress of trying to make friends can cause teens to try unhealthy activities they usually wouldn't try. This is called peer pressure.

Fast Facts

Unhealthy eating patterns can also stem from stress. About 39 percent of U.S. teens skip at least one meal a day due to stress. Another 26 percent say stress makes them overeat or eat more unhealthy foods.

About 31 percent of teens in a study said they felt **overwhelmed** due to stress. Learning to say "no" even when it's hard can help you stay on top of stress.

FAMOUS FACES OF STRESS AND ANXIETY

Many stars are speaking out about dealing with stress and anxiety. Singer Shawn Mendes opened up about his anxiety with the song, "In My Blood." He's said that anxiety hit him when he was around 18. Writing the song helped him, he said, and "it's not all down." The way the song ends shows his strength.

Kristen Bell is another star who's open about her anxiety. She's shared that she's been taking medicine for anxiety and depression since she was young. She's also said talking to a **psychiatrist** and exercising have helped her deal with it.

Shawn Mendes

Kristen Bell

Talking about mental health openly, like Mendes and Bell, is a great way to fight mental health stigma. Stigma involves negative beliefs society may have about something. These beliefs are often unfair and untrue.

Helping a Friend with Anxiety

In social studies class today, the teacher reminded us that we have a test on Thursday. After class, my friend Jacob said he's worried about the test. Our basketball coach told him he needs to get his grades up to stay on the team.

I didn't see Jacob at lunch. I saw him later in the hallway. He looked upset and said nobody saved him a seat at our lunch table. He said he thinks people hate him and he's going to fail our social studies test. I told him that's not true—I enjoy being his friend and will save him a seat from now on. I also said it's OK to feel worried about the test, but I know he's smart and can get a great grade.

> It's a good idea to learn about anxiety if you have a friend who's having a hard time with it. Then you can share what you know! You can find many things to help online, such as this mental health workbook: https://www.cci.health.wa.gov.au/resources/looking-after-yourself.

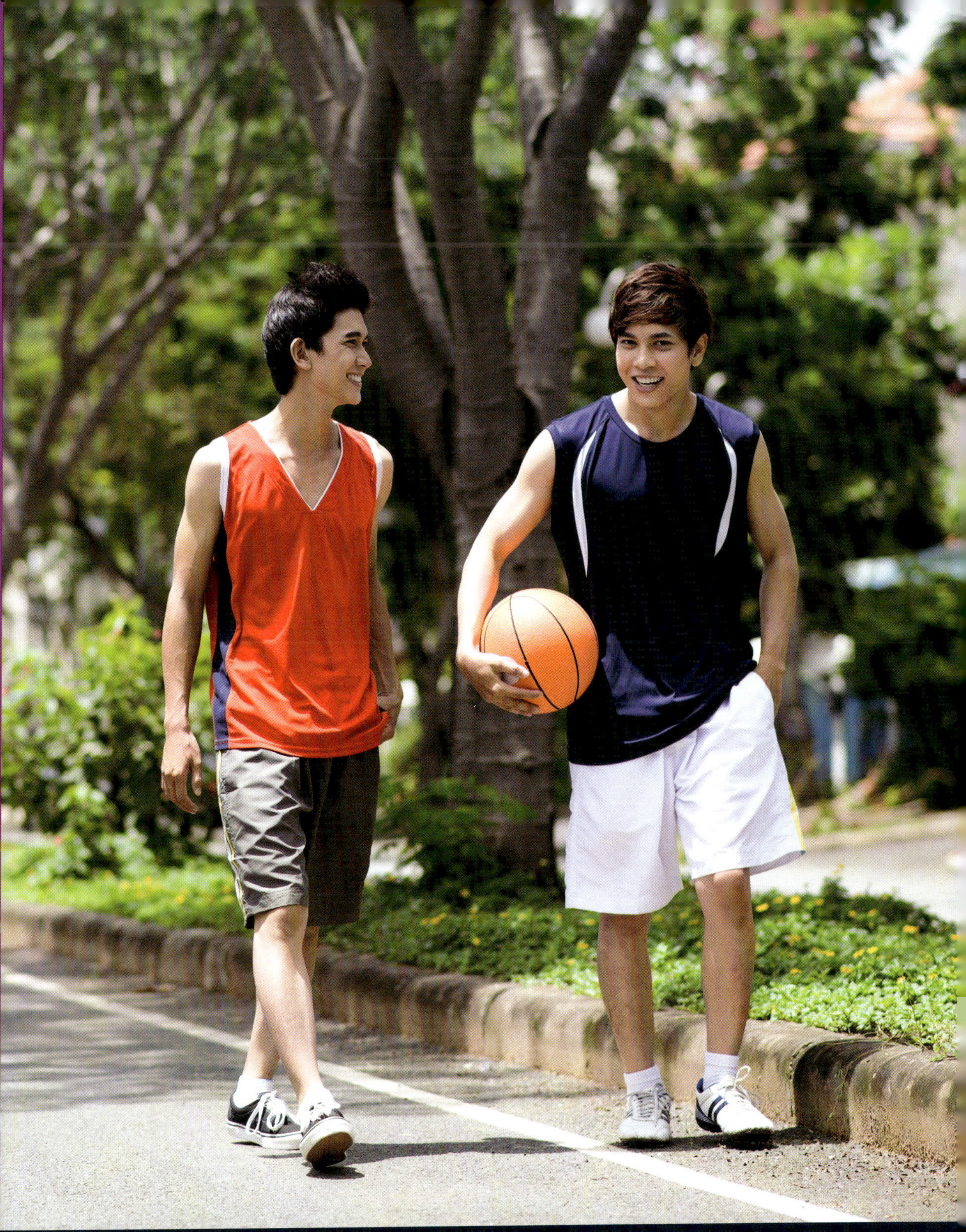

Chapter 2

ANXIETY THROUGH THE YEARS

Diagnosed anxiety disorders haven't been around very long. The American Psychiatric Association (APA) first recognized anxiety disorders in 1980. Before this, it was hard to find treatments for, or ways to manage, stress and anxiety.

DSM stands for *Diagnostic and Statistical Manual of Mental Disorders*. This manual, or guidebook, helps doctors diagnose mental health conditions. There have been five versions, or updated books.

Most anxiety disorders were called "phobias" back then. Today, a phobia is known to be a strong fear of something. Anxiety disorders come in many more types in addition to phobias. Studies and the invention of **psychoanalysis** led to the naming of other specific anxiety disorders.

Fast Facts

Today, around 19 million people in the United States have phobias. These are a type of anxiety disorder.

STRANGE OLD TREATMENTS FOR ANXIETY (#DO NOT TRY!)

- Taking a bath in a very cold river
- Letting leeches suck your blood
- Making your body very hot or very cold

Timeline: Anxiety Through the Years

- 1952: Anxiety is mentioned as a disorder characteristic in *DSM-I*.
- 1970s: Stress and anxiety are seen as phobias.
- 1980: The APA recognizes anxiety disorders.
- 1990: The Phobia Society of America changes its name to Anxiety Disorders Association of America (ADAA).
- 2012: ADAA becomes the Anxiety and Depression Association of America.
- 2013: *DSM-5* includes three different groupings for anxiety.

GENERALIZED ANXIETY DISORDER

One of the most common types of anxiety is generalized anxiety disorder (GAD). A mental health **professional** can diagnose GAD. Someone with GAD often only thinks about the worst things that can happen. These thoughts can make small problems seem much bigger.

> Getting a checkup with a family doctor can be a great place to start in getting help for anxiety. The doctor can look into physical causes of anxiety. They can also recommend a mental health professional.

A doctor can suggest lifestyle changes to help GAD. These can include getting more sleep, doing breathing exercises, and improving **nutrition**. A doctor might also suggest medicine. This is to help balance **chemicals** in the brain.

By the Numbers

About 8 percent of U.S. teens have an anxiety disorder. About 6.8 million people in the United States have GAD.

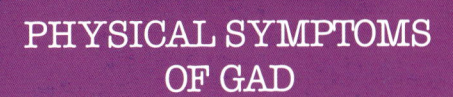

PHYSICAL SYMPTOMS OF GAD

- Tense **muscles**
- Sweating
- Being easily surprised

Things Teens with GAD May Worry About

- Being on time
- Doing well in school, sports, and other activities
- Always fitting in

PANIC DISORDERS

Panic attacks are scary. They can cause racing thoughts and a thumping heart. People with panic disorders often experience panic attacks.

Panic attacks involve the body's built-in "fight or flight" response. This was originally meant to help people survive deadly danger. The body makes a **hormone** called adrenaline when it senses danger. This causes the heart to pump faster.

> Sudden bursts of fear from panic attacks can last a few minutes or longer. When people avoid certain places because of fear of panic attacks, it's called agoraphobia.

Someone with a panic disorder worries about the next panic attack. They often avoid places or things that have caused panic attacks before.

Ways to Help Panic Disorders

- Talk to a doctor about symptoms.
- Learn new ways of thinking, reacting, and behaving with cognitive behavioral therapy (CBT).
- Talk to a doctor about taking a safe medication.

SYMPTOMS OF PANIC ATTACKS

- Racing thoughts
- Pounding heart
- Fearing death
- Dizziness
- Stomach pain
- Trouble breathing
- Sweating
- Feeling out of control
- Chest pain

HELPFUL RESOURCES

Learn more about panic attacks and this type of anxiety from the Child Mind Institute:
https://childmind.org/guide/anxiety-basics/panic-disorder/

OBSESSIVE-COMPULSIVE DISORDER (OCD)

Sometimes it seems bad thoughts take over the mind. This can be a sign of obsessive-compulsive disorder (OCD). This type of anxiety can also lead to behaviors called compulsions. Compulsions can be a way to lower anxious feelings.

Talking to a doctor is the best first step to help OCD. A doctor might then recommend cognitive behavioral therapy, which is often the main treatment. Medication can also help.

Compulsions can be thoughts or actions. Lining up objects and washing hands are actions. Counting in the mind is an example of a mental compulsion. OCD also involves "magical thinking." An example is worrying someone will get hurt or sick due to thoughts or unrelated actions.

Fast Facts

Giving in to compulsions to make anxiety go away is like itching a bug bite. It might feel good at first, but it isn't a long-term fix.

TYPES OF COMPULSIONS

- Cleaning, including washing hands and scrubbing things
- Checking, such as making sure doors are locked multiple times
- Saving, or avoiding throwing anything away
- Repeating, or doing things over again, such as going through a doorway
- Talking, such as asking the same question over and over again
- Arranging, including organizing things so they are in order or in a pattern

SOCIAL ANXIETY

When someone feels like others are always watching or judging them, they may have social anxiety. This type of anxiety stems from any social situation. These can include going on a date and answering a question in class. Even eating in front of people can cause social anxiety.

Social anxiety can get in the way of many everyday things that involve people. These include going to school and work. People may worry for weeks about an event involving other people.

#QUICKQUIZ: SIGNS OF SOCIAL ANXIETY

In the past six months, have you felt:

1. Scared you were being judged by others?
2. Afraid to meet new people?
3. Very unsure of yourself?

If you answered yes to all the above, it might be time to talk to your doctor about your feelings.

Constantly feeling self-conscious, or unsure of oneself, can be a sign of social anxiety. It's important to keep your confidence, or faith in yourself, up. You can do this by believing in yourself and making a list of your accomplishments.

Fast Facts

In 2017, about 9 percent of U.S. teens were living with a social anxiety disorder.

HELPFUL RESOURCE

You can learn more about social anxiety causes and treatment from the National Institute of Mental Health's online downloadable guide: https://www.nimh.nih.gov/health/publications/social-anxiety-disorder-more-than-just-shyness/19-mh-8083-socialanxietydisordermorethanjustshyness_153750.pdf

Chapter 3

Getting Better

I was in my bedroom scrolling through Instagram when I saw it—a picture of my friends at a Billie Eilish concert. I wasn't invited. There "wasn't enough room in the car" for me, they said. I worried it was *really* because my friends think I'm too shy and nervous all the time. Then my phone buzzed with a Snap.

The Snap was from one of my friends at the concert. It showed the huge crowd. I felt so left out.

Tears came to my eyes. But then I followed advice from my counselor. I put down my phone. I picked up my journal and started writing. I felt my sad feelings flow to its pages. I wrote about things I like about myself. Then I realized I don't need those friends to be happy.

FOMO stands for "fear of missing out." When experiencing FOMO, it's important to stay confident, or self-assured. Remember that missing out on something doesn't always matter in the long run.

FINDING PROFESSIONAL HELP

Talking about mental and emotional problems can be hard. But this is an important first step to finding relief and peace. A family doctor could be the first person you share feelings and symptoms with. They can point you in the right direction to find someone with more knowledge on mental health.

> It's important to remember that it might take time to find the right counselor for you. If your mental health isn't getting better, try giving it a month or two. Then you can try finding someone new.

A doctor may send you to a mental health counselor. This kind of counselor helps others with their emotional health. Many counselors have their own practices. However, counselors can also work in schools and hospitals.

Fast Facts

Standing up for your feelings is important. About one in five young people have a mental health condition. However, about half aren't talking about it.

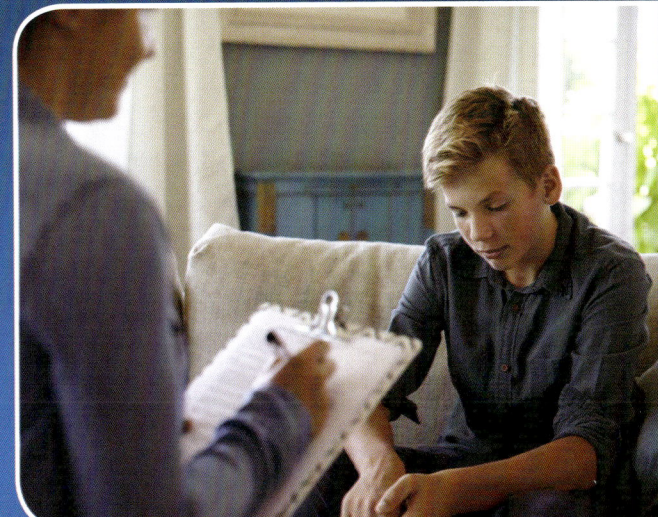

What's the Difference?

Psychologist: A health professional with certain training based on patients and psychological studies of human behavior.

Therapist: Can be a psychologist, social worker, counselor, or another person with special training. Therapists often use more behavior-based ways to help patients.

Counselor: Often have less training than psychologists but may have more methods for helping patients.

SOCIAL ANXIETY SOLUTIONS

Talking to a professional is the best way to get help for social anxiety. However, there are also ways you can cope with negative thoughts yourself.

Challenging negative thoughts such as "I'm going to look so stupid" can be a great first step. Do people *really* think another person is stupid just because they get nervous? No.

Try paying more attention to others. This doesn't mean thinking about what they're thinking. It means paying less attention to your thoughts and feelings for the moment. This can also help in making true connections with other people.

30

Greta Thunberg has a positive outlook about her type of anxiety, which is called selective mutism. This condition often goes hand-in-hand with social anxiety. Greta has used her worries as fuel to make speeches about saving the planet.

OTHER TIPS TO TAKE ON SOCIAL ANXIETY

- Stay in the present moment. Try not to think about the future or past mistakes.
- Pay as much attention as possible to what others are saying.
- Remember that you don't have to be perfect—nobody is.
- Slow down your breathing.

HELPFUL RESOURCE

Check out this online guide that uses cognitive behavioral therapy to help social anxiety symptoms: https://www.nhsinform.scot/illnesses-and-conditions/mental-health/mental-health-self-help-guides/social-anxiety-self-help-guide

TAKING ON TECHNOLOGY

Teen smartphone ownership has exploded in recent years. In 2012, less than half of all teens owned a smartphone. In 2018, 89 percent did.

Studies have found that smartphones and social media can cause stress and anxiety. Teens can feel left out of events their friends post about on social media. About one in 10 teens in 2018 also reported they'd been cyberbullied. Cyberbullying is bullying through **technology**.

Cyberbullying causes people to feel hurt and powerless. Having to deal with cyberbullying adds stress to people's lives. They can also feel less confident, which makes mental health problems more likely.

TEXT ANXIETY

Texting and using social media can make it harder to speak face-to-face with people. Many people worry teens aren't building important social skills. This can lead to more cases of social anxiety.

HOBBIES FOR HEALING

Stress and anxiety can make negative thoughts powerful. Hobbies are a great way to take your attention off troubling thoughts. This can ease other symptoms too.

There are many hobbies to choose from. Cooking and crafting can allow you to create something rewarding while easing your mind. Writing lets you get thoughts out of your head and onto paper. Exercise, such as running or yoga, might be most helpful. Exercise causes the body to make effective feel-good hormones called endorphins.

Love animals? You're in luck! Petting and playing with animals eases stress. It causes the body to make oxytocin, a hormone that lowers stress. It's also called the "cuddle hormone" because it can help us bond with others.

FINDING PEACE WITH GOOD EATS

What you eat—or don't eat—can really affect how you feel. Studies have found that food can both cause and help anxiety and stress.

While it might seem like a good idea to skip a meal if you're busy, don't. This can cause your blood sugar to drop, making you feel shaky. This can worsen anxiety.

Cooking may be one of the best stress relievers. Chopping, tasting, and smelling can keep you in the present moment. This keeps your attention from negative thoughts. It can also help you eat healthier. This controls stress too.

Complex carbohydrates, such as bread and pasta, can make you calmer. That's because they can make your blood sugar level more even. Sugary foods can make anxiety worse because they can make blood sugar levels rise or fall faster.

FEEL-GOOD FOODS

FOODS	NUTRIENTS
avocados and almonds	High in vitamin B, which causes the body to make feel-good hormones.
Alaskan salmon	Contains omega-3 fatty acids, which lower anxiety.
beef, egg yolks, oysters, cashews	Rich in zinc, which eases anxiety.
pickles, sauerkraut, and kefir	These foods are rich in probiotics, which have good bacteria for your body, which can help with social anxiety.

Wonderful Water

Drinks such as coffee and soda have caffeine. Caffeine is a chemical that can cause anxiety. Water is a much better choice!

SECURING SLEEP

Your brain needs sleep like your body needs food. Not sleeping enough can cause stress and anxiety. It can also make other problems worse.

If you have trouble falling asleep, a doctor can help you find treatments. A mental health professional may suggest cognitive behavioral therapy. This would help you learn what thoughts and behaviors are causing you to lose sleep.

There are also things you can do at home. Try avoiding looking at a phone, TV, or computer before bed. This prepares your mind for sleep.

Catch Those Zzzzs

About 35 percent of teens say stress causes them to lay awake at night. Losing sleep can make it harder to learn and pay attention. This can lead to problems in school.

Meditation may be your secret to falling asleep. It involves paying attention to your breathing. You also picture a peaceful place, like a sunny field, in your mind.

TAKE CONTROL OF YOUR TIME

A lot of stress and anxiety may stem from feeling like you don't have control over your life. Time management is a way for you to take back that control.

Time management is being careful about how you spend your time. It starts with being honest with yourself about your time. It's also a good idea to figure out what's really important to you. What are your goals? What can you do to meet these goals? This might mean giving up things that are less important.

TIME MANAGEMENT

OBJECTIVE • PRIORITY • SCHEDULE • REMINDER • EFFICIENCY • ALERTS • CONTROLLING

When planning your time, it's important to remember you can always reach out for help. Also, it's a good idea to plan time each day for some **relaxation**. This can even be time to just do nothing!

TIME MANAGEMENT STEPS

- Make sure you fully understand what's involved in all of your responsibilities.
- Make a checklist of everything you need to get done.
- Come up with a plan or extra time for things that might slow down one or more of your tasks.
- Plan out the steps using a calendar, planner, or another tool.
- Track how long it takes to do each task.
- Use tracked times to plan future projects.

Chapter 4

STANDING UP TO STIGMA

Once you discover the mental health help you need, there's more you can do. You can talk openly about mental health issues. This can **inspire** others to get help.

Many people don't understand mental health conditions. Some think stress and anxiety are easy to control.

You can help others learn this isn't true. You can also teach others not to use words such as "crazy," "nuts," or "OCD" in bad or wrong ways. Stress and anxiety can affect us all. It's key that we share our stories so we can all live more stress-free lives.

STRESS FREE ZONE

World Mental Health Day is October 10. Many famous people, such as Great Britain's Prince Harry, mark this day. You can mark the days with United States-based groups such as Mental Health America (MHA) and the National Alliance on Mental Illness (NAMI).

Overcoming

I smiled as I read the grade on my most recent math test: A.

I got a C on the test I didn't finish earlier in the year. I'm thankful Olivia talked with me about her stress and anxiety. I found a counselor who's been really helpful. She's taught me how to make sure I plan out my time and get enough sleep. I gave up a few after-school activities, but it's been worth it!

I've made time for a new calming hobby—yoga. I go to classes with Olivia. Together we're also helping others learn about the importance of taking care of their mental health. It feels like my negative experience is now helping others. Honestly, I think that's way better than any test grade!

Healthy friendships are key for mental well-being. They can inspire you to be more self-assured. Check out a mental health first aid course to learn how you can help a friend in need: www.mentalhealthfirstaid.org/take-a-course.

GLOSSARY

challenge: Something that is hard to do; also, to confront or question someone or something.
chemical: Matter that can be mixed with other matter to cause changes.
cognitive: Related to brain activities such as thinking, remembering, or reasoning.
depression: A serious medical condition in which a person has strong sad feelings.
diagnose: To identify a disease by its signs or symptoms.
digestive: Having to do with the body parts concerned with eating, breaking down, and taking in food.
hormone: A chemical made in the body that tells another part of the body what to do.
inspire: To cause someone to want to do something.
muscle: A part of the body that produces motion.
natural: Determined by nature; normal.
nutrition: The process of eating the right food to grow and be healthy.
overwhelmed: A feeling of having too much to deal with.
performance: An activity before a group of people.

professional: Someone who does a certain job for a living.
psychiatrist: A person who practices a branch of medicine that deals with mental, behavioral, or emotional disorders.
psychoanalysis: A way of treating a mental health condition that involves a patient talking about thoughts, feelings, dreams, and memories.
psychologist: A person who studies psychology, or the science or study of the mind and behavior.
relationship: A connection to another person.
relaxation: Spending time resting and doing something fun.
subconscious: Happening in a part of the mind that people aren't aware of.
technology: The way people do something using tools and the tools that they use.

INDEX

A
adrenaline, 20
agoraphobia, 20
American Psychiatric Association (APA), 16, 17
Anxiety and Depression Association of America, 17
anxiety disorder, 9, 16, 17, 19, 25
Anxiety Disorders Association of America (ADAA), 17

B
Bell, Kristen, 12, 13
blood sugar, 37

C
cognitive behavioral therapy (CBT), 21, 22, 31, 38
compulsions, 22, 23
counselor, 28, 29, 44
cyberbullying, 32, 33

D
depression, 9, 12
Diagnostic and Statistical Manual of Mental Disorders (DSM), 16, 17
digestive issues, 6

E
exercises/exercising, 12, 34

F
financial problems, 7

G
generalized anxiety disorder (GAD), 18, 19

H
headaches, 9
heart, 20, 21

M
medication/medicine, 12, 19, 21, 22
meditation, 39
memory, 6
Mendes, Shawn, 12, 13
Mental Health America (MHA), 43

N
National Alliance on Mental Illness (NAMI), 43
National Institute of Mental Health, 25
nutrition, 19

O
obsessive-compulsive disorder, (OCD), 22, 23, 42

P
panic attacks, 20, 21
panic disorders, 20, 21
phobias, 17
Phobia Society of America, 17
psychiatrist, 12
psychoanalysis, 17
psychologist, 4, 29

S
school, 7, 8, 19, 24, 29, 38, 44
sleep, 6, 9, 19, 38
social anxiety, 24, 25, 30, 31, 33
social media, 32, 33
stigma, 13
stomachaches, 9
symptoms, 6, 19, 21, 28

T
tests, 4, 5, 6, 14, 44
therapist, 29
Thunberg, Greta, 31
time management, 40, 41

W
World Mental Health Day, 43